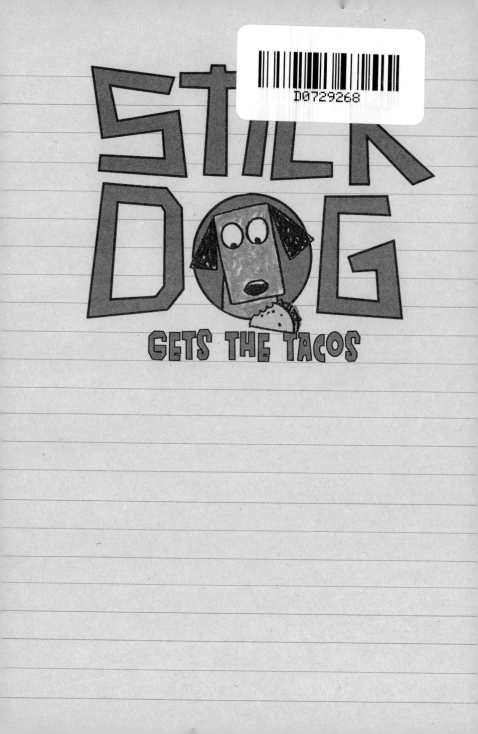

STICK DOG

GETS THE TACOS

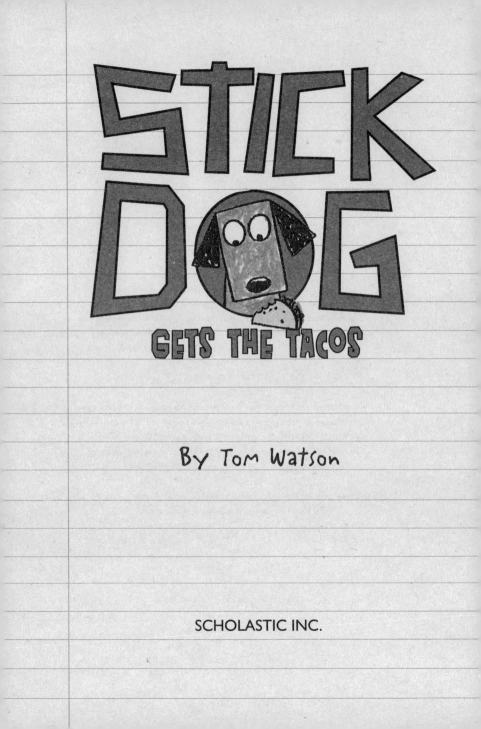

STICK DOG

GETS THE TACOS

By Tom Watson

SCHOLASTIC INC.

ISBN 978-1-338-59720-2

Copyright © 2019 by Tom Watson. Illustrations by Ethan Long based on original sketches by Tom Watson. All rights reserved. Published by Scholastic Inc., 557 Broadway, New York, NY 10012, by arrangement with HarperCollins Children's Books, a division of HarperCollins Publishers. SCHOLASTIC and associated logos are trademarks and/or registered trademarks of Scholastic Inc.

The publisher does not have any control over and does not assume any responsibility for author or third-party websites or their content.

12 11 10 9 8 7 6 5 4 3 2 1   20 21 22 23 24 25

Printed in the U.S.A.   40

First Scholastic printing, January 2020

Typography by Honee Jang

Dedicated to MEJ

(IWTASD)

TABLE OF CONTENTS

CHAPTER 1

A VERY SHORT NAP

In the late afternoon, Stick Dog rested in his pipe under Highway 16. His eyelids hung halfway down. He was tired from an unsuccessful food search during the day.

He looked around at Mutt, Poo-Poo, and Stripes. They were on their bellies. Their eyes were closed.

Only Karen was missing.

But Stick Dog knew exactly where she was—and he was not concerned about her at all.

Karen was at Picasso Park. She had veered off as they all sulked back from behind the mall an hour ago. Karen craved barbecue potato chips—her favorite treat—and wanted to check for some at her lucky garbage can.

Stick Dog's eyes drooped even farther. They were now just slits. He tried to stay awake to welcome Karen. He knew she would arrive soon.

But it was too difficult.

His eyes shut completely.

And Stick Dog fell instantly and deeply asleep.

But only for twenty-seven seconds.

That's because after twenty-seven seconds, Karen sprinted into Stick Dog's pipe—and Stick Dog heard her rapid approach.

She stopped the best she could, but her speed and momentum were too much. She slammed into Stick Dog's side, waking him instantly from his twenty-seven-second slumber.

Stick Dog opened his eyes. Karen's face was right in front of his.

She panted quickly. Her eyes stretched wide open.

Stick Dog smiled at Karen.

Karen smiled at Stick Dog.

She asked him, "Did you have a nice nap?"

"I did," Stick Dog said kindly. There was no reason to tell Karen that he had been asleep for less than a minute. "Thank you for asking. What have you been up to?"

"Big stuff, Stick Dog, big stuff," Karen said. "I made two super-important discoveries."

BIG STUFF!

"You did?"

"I did."

"Would you like to tell me about them?"

Karen nodded her head very quickly. She was eager to tell him.

What Stick Dog didn't know at the time was that Karen's two discoveries were two very different things.

One was amusing.

And the other was alarming.

CHAPTER 2

IS KAREN GETTING TALLER?

Stick Dog asked, "What is your first discovery?"

"It's something amazing. Truly amazing," Karen said. "But first, can I ask you something?"

"Of course."

"Do you think I'm gaining speed?" asked Karen. There was a hint of excitement and pride in her voice. "You know, getting faster?"

Stick Dog was not certain what this line of inquiry had to do with Karen's discovery, but he thought addressing it quickly was probably the best course of action.

"I'm not sure," he said. "Maybe so. I've always thought of you as pretty darn fast. Why do you ask?"

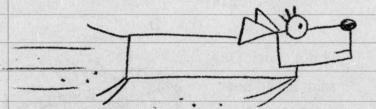

Karen didn't answer for a few seconds. She glanced about at Mutt, Stripes, and Poo-Poo. They were all still fast asleep. This seemed to satisfy Karen. She lowered her voice when she offered her answer.

"I think my legs are getting longer," Karen said in a confiding near-whisper. "I think I'm getting taller. That's the first discovery!"

Now, this response caught Stick Dog by surprise. Karen was fully grown, he knew that. He asked, "Why do you think your legs are getting longer?"

"Do you remember that big storm we had last week?" Karen asked in reply. "That's when I got my proof."

"I do," Stick Dog said. It had been a loud and fierce storm with plenty of lightning and thunderclaps. "It was really coming down."

"And then it cleared up and the sun came out and it got super-hot really fast," Karen said. "Do you remember that?"

Stick Dog nodded. It had indeed been a big storm—and a hot, hot day.

"Well, after the storm I got really warm," Karen went on. "I was near Picasso Park and there are always such great puddles there after it rains. So I found a nice, deep puddle by the picnic tables. Do you know where I mean?"

"Yes," Stick Dog confirmed. "There are nice puddles there."

"Right, right," Karen said. She was glad that Stick Dog was following along. "Well, I stepped right into the middle of that puddle to cool down. And guess what?"

"What?"

"The water came up over my knees, that's
what."

Karen seemed to be done now. And Stick
Dog hadn't yet understood how this proved
she was getting taller.

"I see," he said. "And, umm, how does that
prove your legs are growing?"

Karen squinted one eye and nodded. "There's
more to the story."

"I bet there is," said Stick Dog. "Let's hear it."

"After I cooled off," continued Karen. Her
voice had risen a bit now and her words came
faster. She was growing excited. "I fell asleep
under one of the picnic tables. It was shady

there and way cooler than out in the bright sun. I slept for at least a couple of hours."

Stick Dog now had an idea where this might all be going, but he didn't say anything. He listened intently as Karen went on.

"When I woke up," she said, speaking even faster now, "I was hot again. So I went back to that same puddle. And guess what?"

"What?" asked Stick Dog, even though he knew what was coming.

"When I stood in that puddle the second time," Karen answered quickly. She was hopping up and down a little bit now. "The puddle was only up to my ankles!"

Stick Dog pressed his lips together. He said nothing.

"Don't you see?" Karen asked. Her tail wagged like mad now. "My legs grew while I was asleep! The water only came up to my ankles in the exact same puddle!"

Stick Dog nodded but was silent. It looked

like he was attempting to find something
to say.

"And if I'm getting faster, then that proves
it even more!" Karen exclaimed. "If my legs
are longer, then I can cover more ground
with each step! Faster means bigger!"

Stick Dog continued to nod and think.
He knew that Karen was thrilled with the
prospect of growing bigger. He also knew
that, in fact, she wasn't growing bigger. And
Stick Dog had no interest in explaining what
the passage of time and a hot day could do
to a puddle. He knew that Karen had not
grown taller—he knew
that the puddle had
become more shallow.

"It's exciting,
isn't it?!" Karen

asked. "I mean, just imagine if I grew up to be as big as you or Mutt or Stripes or Poo-Poo! That would be awesome!"

Stick Dog nodded slowly, but he didn't speak. Instead, he allowed the shadow of a frown to come forward on his face. He didn't look angry or disappointed— just a little bit sad.

And Karen noticed.

"What is it, Stick Dog?" she asked. There was concern on her face—and any trace of excitement was gone now. "What's the matter?"

"It would just make me sad if you grew to our size, that's all," he answered.

"Why?"

"You're so unique," Stick Dog said. "You're so different in so many ways. We all are. Having differences is the best—the absolute best. It makes us a great team. It would be totally boring if we all looked and acted the same. Our differences are what make us strong."

Karen cocked her head sideways a bit. And Stick Dog tried to explain further.

He asked, "What's special about Mutt?"

Karen looked over at Mutt. His front paws were folded beneath his chin as he slept. "He's shaggy," observed Karen.

"Right," Stick Dog said, and smiled. "And

his shagginess means he can store things in his fur. Those things often serve as tools to help us snatch food. Remember the nail we used to give that worker a flat tire so we could get the donuts?"

Karen nodded and licked her lips. She remembered the sweet doughy goodness of donuts.

"And what's special about Poo-Poo?"

"He likes to bash his head into things— on purpose."

"That's definitely unique," Stick Dog said. "And his head-bashing prowess has toppled a lot of garbage cans where we've found a lot of tasty scraps, hasn't it?"

Karen nodded again.

"And what about Stripes?"

"She's the fastest."

"She's totally fast," confirmed Stick Dog. "Remember when she saw those witches and ran away—and warned us? That was really important."

Karen looked up at Stick Dog. Her tail was wagging again now. She looked down at herself. She peered back up at Stick Dog and said, "And I'm short."

She then waited eagerly to see what Stick Dog would say about her.

"You're a little smaller than us, it's true," Stick Dog said. "And you were the only one who could fit under that Dumpster and discover the spaghetti in that container. We would have never had that spaghetti feast without you."

"And I was the only one who could fit my head into that coffee cup," Karen offered. "Do you remember that?"

"I do."

"I did it a couple of times."

"I remember."

"I couldn't have done that if I was big."

"That's true."

"I really like coffee."

"I know you do."

"I mean, I LOVE, LOVE, LOVE coffee!"

"Maybe we'll find some more someday,"
Stick Dog said, and smiled down at Karen.

Her eyes glistened now, her tail wagged, and her little dachshund chest was puffed up a bit. He concluded, "So, it's really nice that you're smaller, I think."

"I actually hope I'm *not* growing."

"Who knows? Maybe you're not, after all."

"Stick Dog?" Karen asked.

"Yes?"

"What's special about you?"

"Oh, I don't know," answered Stick Dog modestly. "Not so much."

Karen thought about her own question for a while. Her face got all scrunched up in thought as she concentrated for a few moments. Then she came up with an answer. Her face unscrunched and a satisfied little grin came to her face.

"I figured out what's special about you."

"You did?" Stick Dog asked. He looked forward to Karen's answer. Everyone likes to get a compliment now and then, after all. "What's that?"

"You're not as smart as the rest of us," Karen said.

NOT SMART.

Stick Dog paused then. He felt a laugh building up in his belly, and he did his best to suppress it. "Is that right?"

"I think so, yes," Karen said. "It's okay if you don't understand quite what I'm saying. That's just normal for you. Not understanding things is what makes you special."

"Well," Stick Dog said. He was confident now that he had stifled the laugh inside his belly. "I've never thought of myself like that before."

"Not thinking of things just comes naturally to you, I guess."

Stick Dog, while amused and enjoying this back-and-forth conversation with Karen, was now ready to move on. He asked, "What is your second discovery?"

When Karen answered his question, Stick Dog wished they hadn't spent so much time talking about Karen getting taller.

Her second discovery was more than just a discovery.

It was an emergency.

And Stick Dog had to help.

CHAPTER 3

WAKE UP!

"A second discovery?" asked Karen.

"When you ran in here earlier, you said there were two super-important discoveries," Stick Dog reminded her. "You must have seen or heard something on the way back here from Picasso Park."

"Didn't I come back with you guys?" asked Karen sincerely. Her forehead was wrinkled and she stared at the ceiling of Stick Dog's pipe.

"We were all together for a while," Stick Dog answered. "But about halfway back, you decided to go to Picasso Park by yourself. You wanted to check your favorite garbage can for food."

"That's right, I did," Karen confirmed. She remembered now. "I love that garbage can! Sometimes I even find barbecue potato chips!"

"I know you do," Stick Dog said politely. "Did you make it to your favorite garbage can?"

"No."

"What happened before you got there?"

"A bunch of stuff happened."

"Like what?"

"I saw a ladybug. That's one thing."

"That probably wasn't the second discovery. We've seen ladybugs before."

"No, probably not. But I do love ladybugs! Did you know they have black spots?"

"I did know that."

"I thought maybe with your lack of smarts, you might not know that ladybugs have black spots."

"I see," Stick Dog said, and paused. Then he asked, "What happened after you saw the ladybug?"

"I took a nap under the slide for a few minutes."

"That probably wasn't the second discovery."

"I don't think so either," Karen replied. "But it was nice and cool under there. Did you know it's cooler in the shade than out in the bright, hot sunshine?"

"I know that too."

"Good for you," Karen said. "That's real, real smart of you, Stick Dog."

"Umm, thanks," answered Stick Dog as genuinely as he could. "What did you do when you woke up under the slide? What happened next?"

Karen squeezed her eyes shut to help her think.

Her body began to shiver.

"That's it," she whispered. "I saw it with my own two eyes. It was terrible, Stick Dog. It might still be happening."

Stick Dog kept his voice calm and steady. He asked, "What was it?"

Karen shook her head.

"You can tell me."

She shook her head again.

"Maybe we can help."

This was the nudge of encouragement Karen needed. She took one step closer to Stick Dog. Her body continued to tremble.

"It was after I left Picasso Park. I was on my way here and I took the shortcut by that house between the park and the woods," Karen whispered, her eyes now wide open.

Stick Dog knew that house. He and his

friends had often snuck past it to get to the woods. He nodded for her to continue.

"That's where I saw it. In the backyard."

She stopped then, squeezed her eyes shut again, and shook her head.

"What did you see?"

"I can't."

"Yes, you can."

Karen opened her eyes and stared directly into Stick Dog's eyes. He held his stare steady on her.

"Go on," encouraged Stick Dog. He could tell something was truly wrong. "It's okay."

Karen whispered, "In that backyard. Under a big oak tree. They were hitting a . . . a . . . a . . ."

"A what, Karen?" Stick Dog asked. "They were hitting a what?"

Karen closed her eyes again and answered. "A dog," she said. "They were hitting a dog."

The words took only two seconds to register with Stick Dog. And when they did, his face grew fierce. His shoulder muscles tensed. His lips quivered and a snarl began to take shape on his mouth.

He knew there was no time to waste.

He shouted one thing.

And one thing only.

"Wake up!"

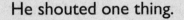

Never in all their time together had Karen, Poo-Poo, Mutt, and Stripes ever heard such a shout from Stick Dog. He was loud—and he was angry.

Karen jumped back from the sheer volume and ferocity of the sound.

Stripes, Mutt, and Poo-Poo were instantly

awake—and instantly up on their paws.
They asked in unison, "What is it?!"

"Something terrible!" Stick Dog screamed
as he sprinted toward the opening of his
pipe. "Near the house at the edge of the
woods! A dog's in trouble! Karen saw it!
We have to help! Follow me! Karen will
explain the details on the way!"

Nobody responded as Stick Dog leaped out
of his pipe.

But they did follow him as fast as they
could.

CHAPTER 4

QUESTIONS

Stick Dog was cautious and practical in all things. He had to be to keep this gang of strays safe—and fed. He had learned the value of good, smart, secure planning—and carefully executed action.

But he exercised no caution now.

Poo-Poo, Mutt, Stripes, and Karen had never seen Stick Dog run so fast. He hurdled over fallen limbs and branches in the forest. He thrust and pushed through brush they normally went around. He took the fastest, straightest path toward that house at the forest's edge.

The others did their best to keep up, but even Stripes—usually the fastest of the five dogs—couldn't do it. Stick Dog was out of sight in just a couple of minutes.

While they hustled after him, Mutt, Poo-Poo, and Stripes attempted to get more information from Karen.

"What's going . . . on?" Stripes shouted and panted as they ran. "What did . . . you see?"

Karen churned her little dachshund legs as fast as she could. Despite her efforts, she was slowly losing ground to the others. And she was definitely far behind—and way out of earshot—of Stick Dog.

"Some humans . . . were . . . hurting . . . a dog," Karen called ahead to Stripes as best she could. She was panting even more than the others.

"How?" Mutt asked from ahead.

"They were . . . hitting . . . it," Karen answered.

Anger and dismay came to all their faces as they ran. They could barely believe what they heard. And they began to run—and pant—even harder.

Poo-Poo called back, "What . . . were . . . they . . . hitting it . . . with?"

"A . . . stick," Karen called forward. She had fallen even further behind.

"Who . . . was . . . doing it?" Stripes yelled.

"Little . . . humans," Karen called meekly back. She was almost completely out of breath now.

Mutt asked a final question. They were almost to the edge of the woods now—almost to that house. It would only be a minute or two more. They knew that Stick Dog, in fact, was probably already there.

Mutt asked, "Where . . . was . . . the . . . dog?"

Karen took the deepest breath she could. She called, "In . . . a . . . tree."

CHAPTER 5

STRIPES VERSUS A TREE

At hearing Karen's answer, Mutt, Stripes, and Poo-Poo all skidded to a stop in the forest. Their paws sprayed small clouds of leaves, twigs, and dirt all around them.

They looked back at Karen. She was twenty yards away and working hard to catch up.

"Did she . . . say . . . the dog . . . was in . . . a tree?" Mutt asked Poo-Poo and Stripes.

They nodded and panted hard to catch their breath.

"Can . . . dogs . . . climb trees?" Mutt asked.

Stripes and Poo-Poo shook their heads.

Karen was almost to them now.

"Are you . . . sure?" asked Mutt.

After a minute, everyone—well, everyone except Karen, who had just arrived to join the others—could breathe almost normally.

"I'm fairly certain that . . . dogs cannot climb trees," Stripes said. "Do you know how I know?"

"How?" Mutt asked.

"I've never seen . . . a dog . . . climb a tree, that's how," answered Stripes confidently.

Poo-Poo nodded his agreement and added his own unique perspective.

"If dogs could climb trees," he chimed in. He had caught his breath fully. "I would have defeated hundreds—probably thousands— of squirrels by now. Those whisker-twitching, nut-munching demons would be practically extinct if the fierce and powerful Mister Poo-Poo could climb trees. Without a doubt."

Poo-Poo puffed out his chest and waited for confirmation from his friends.

While he waited, Stripes contemplated the

whole "can-dogs-climb-trees?" question quite seriously. She was, by chance, standing next to a tall oak tree. Stripes looked at it from the base of its trunk to the top of its tallest branch. She examined the width and girth of its dark green canopy.

"I don't *think* I can climb a tree," Stripes said—more to herself than to the others. The subject now seemed to intrigue her immensely. She took two steps backward. "But I guess I've never *really* tried."

With that said, Stripes took one small step for dogs—and one giant leap for dogkind.

She landed with all four paws simultaneously on the oak tree's vertical trunk. Instantly, she scrambled and churned her legs to move up the big oak's trunk.

She fell down.

Karen, Poo-Poo, and Mutt all watched
this without comment. They were busy.
Mutt had shaken an old gardening glove
from his fur and gnawed on it slowly and
rhythmically. Karen was still catching her
breath. And Poo-Poo continued to wait for
the others to confirm that squirrels would
be nearly extinct if he had tree-climbing
powers.

Stripes had another idea.

She stood on her back
paws and stretched her
front legs forward as far
as she could. Then, with
an energetic little leap,

Stripes sprang into the air and wrapped all four legs around the trunk in a tree-hugging position. She shimmied her whole body upward, jerking her hips and shoulders a couple of times. It sort of looked like she was a white, eighty-pound inchworm with black spots.

Then she slid down to the ground.

As she did, Mutt chewed, Karen panted, and Poo-Poo waited.

Stripes stood and shook, spraying tiny chunks of tree bark from her fur.

She had one more idea.

This time, Stripes sat down next to the tree. She leaned her back against it, wriggling a bit

until she was comfortable. And then Stripes
did—and said—a most unusual thing.

She closed her eyes, raised her paws to
both sides of her forehead, and began to
speak.

"I am up in the tree. I am up in the tree.
I am up in the tree," she chanted quietly.
"I am up in the tree. I am up in the tree.
I am up in the tree."

After a full minute of this, Stripes slowly opened her eyes. You could kind of tell that she expected to be buried among the leaves and branches high up in that oak tree. Her eyes darted left and right, up and down.

You might be surprised to learn that Stripes was not, in fact, up in the tree.

She was on the ground.

"It's no use," she announced to Mutt, Poo-Poo, and Karen. "I've tried everything I can think of. And dogs cannot climb trees."

"I know that for sure," confirmed Poo-Poo. "Because squirrels still exist. If I could climb trees, then there wouldn't be a squirrel around here for miles and miles."

Again, Poo-Poo waited for confirmation from his friends. He probably would have continued to wait for some time.

But something happened just then.

Stick Dog came back.

CHAPTER 6

IT'S NOT A DOG

When Stick Dog emerged through some thick brush, his friends immediately stopped what they were doing. They wanted to know what he had discovered at the house near the edge of the forest.

Mutt tucked the old gardening glove back into his fur. Karen had caught her breath now. Poo-Poo had quickly forgotten about

squirrels. And Stripes gladly moved away
from the big oak tree and toward Stick Dog.

"Did you see it?!" Karen asked first. "Did
you see the humans hurting that dog?"

"Yes," answered Stick Dog. "But it's not
quite—"

Stripes interrupted then.

She asked, "Is the dog in a tree? For real?
Because I'm pretty sure dogs cannot climb
trees."

"It *is* in a tree," Stick Dog said. "Sort of.
You see, what Karen saw—"

This time Poo-Poo interrupted.

"If we could climb trees," he said with tremendous confidence, "squirrels probably wouldn't exist anymore. I would have taken care of that entire chattering, puffy-tailed population once and for all."

"I'm certain that's true," Stick Dog said, and nodded. "Well, I'm sure you'd all like to know what I discovered at—"

"Stick Dog?"

It was Mutt.

"Yes?"

"I apologize for interrupting."

"It's okay."

"It's just that I made a discovery myself," Mutt said. Whatever he was about to say seemed very important to him. Mutt rarely interrupted his friends.

"What did you discover, Mutt?" asked Stick Dog.

"I discovered," replied Mutt, "that I really like chewing on gloves more than mittens. You wouldn't think there would be much difference. But, brother, there is. I think it's the fingers. Those dangly, flexible things feel so good between my teeth. With mittens, it's just the whole big bunchy thing. But not with gloves, man. Not with gloves!"

Stick Dog smiled at this. He seemed totally at ease—the exact opposite of the way he looked and felt several minutes ago when he sprinted off to investigate Karen's "emergency."

"Do you guys want to know what I found out?" Stick Dog asked his friends.

They all did.

"Karen was right," Stick Dog partially acknowledged. "There are, in fact, some small humans hitting a dog—in a tree. Only it's not a dog. It's a unicorn. And it's not real. It's like a toy or something."

"It's not real?" Karen asked. You could hear honest relief in her voice. "It's not alive?"

"No. It's not real," confirmed Stick Dog. "It's not alive."

"It's not a dog?" Karen asked. She needed further proof that this was not, indeed, an emergency.

"It's not a dog," answered Stick Dog. "It's shaped like a horse."

"When I saw it, I thought it was a horse-shaped dog," Karen explained.

"It has a horn," added Stick Dog.

"I thought it was a horse-shaped dog with a horn."

Stick Dog said, "It's covered in sparkles."

"I thought it was a horse-shaped dog with a horn covered in sparkles."

"It's decorated with rainbows."

"I thought it was a horse-shaped dog with a horn covered in sparkles that, umm—" Karen said, and then stopped. "I didn't notice the rainbows, I guess."

"I can totally understand how you thought it was a dog," Stick Dog reassured Karen. He wanted to help her feel better about her mistake. "When I saw that sparkly, rainbow-covered, horse-shaped toy, I thought just one thing for a moment."

"What did you think?" asked Karen.

"I thought it was a dog hanging on a string from a tree."

"I'm sure you did," Karen said. She seemed relieved. "It's probably a very common mistake."

Stick Dog smiled at her—and then moved on to the main subject.

"I've got good news for you guys," Stick Dog said. He grinned at them—and waited.

"What is it, Stick Dog?" Stripes yelped. She was not very patient. She jumped up into the air, landed, and then spun around twice, kicking a few big brown pinecones as she did. "What is it?!"

"I think," Stick Dog responded slowly, "there's going to be a picnic."

"Where?!" screamed Poo-Poo.

"I'll show you," Stick Dog said. "Come on!"

CHAPTER 7

BIRDIE-ATTACKING RAMPAGE

"There," Stick Dog said, and pointed after they got to the edge of the forest. They nestled and hid behind a tangle of honeysuckle bushes and cattail reeds. Behind them was a huge pine tree. They began to observe their surroundings. "That's where I think the picnic will be."

There was a patio at the back of the house. A boy and girl were there. On the patio was a picnic table and benches. A huge umbrella with an orange canopy stood over the table. There was a grill, which was not in use, a couple of chairs, and a big maple tree with the unicorn hanging from it.

"Stick Dog!" Karen yelped suddenly, and pointed at the boy and the girl. "Those small humans are hitting the dog again! With that stick!"

"It's not a dog, Karen," Stick Dog said. "Remember? It's a unicorn. And it's not alive. And unicorns aren't real."

"Oh, right," Karen said quickly, instantly relieved. "But they *are* hitting it again."

Stick Dog looked toward the maple tree.
Those two little humans were, indeed,
hitting the unicorn again. They laughed
and took turns wrapping a cloth around
their heads to cover their eyes—and then
whacked the unicorn with the stick.

They were probably a brother and a
sister—and they had very little success
striking the unicorn. The girl hit it twice in a

row—but both times were glancing blows, merely pushing the unicorn aside so that it swung around a bit. The boy swung three times but missed every time.

It was an odd ritual. Stick Dog had certainly never seen humans act in such a bizarre way before.

"They seem really, really mad at that unicorn," Stripes said. "I wonder why. I mean, it doesn't seem to be bothering anybody. It's just hanging in that tree minding its own business. I don't really see the need to go bashing it about like that."

Stick Dog said, "I think it's probably some sort of game or some—"

But he stopped.

Right then two large humans, one male and one female, stepped out of the home's back door.

"Okay, you guys. Time to stop," the big female human said. "You're not supposed to hit the piñata yet. You can do that after dinner."

The big male human agreed. He said, "After dinner is right—and after the game. Game first, dinner after, then the piñata. That's the deal."

The boy untied and unwrapped the cloth from his head. He blinked a few times to adjust to the late afternoon sunlight.

"But I'm hungry now," he pleaded to his mom.

I'M HUNGRY NOW.

"You'll have to wait," she said. "The tacos aren't even here yet. You two go warm up. We'll set the table and be right there."

The dad agreed again. As he pushed the back of his hands in the air in a shooing motion, he said, "Good idea. Get a little practice in. It's going to be parents versus kids. We've won three in a row—you need all the help you can get. Go hit the birdie."

As soon as the words were out of the big male's mouth, Karen, Poo-Poo, Stripes, and Mutt all looked at Stick Dog. Stripes spoke for the group.

"First they hit a dog with a stick," Stripes said, aghast. "And now they're going to start hitting harmless little birdies!"

"That's terrible!" Mutt exclaimed angrily while Poo-Poo and Karen snarled their own disapproval.

"It wasn't a dog," Stick Dog said calmly, and pointed toward the tree. "It was a unicorn. A fake unicorn. Remember?"

"Whatever," Stripes said. She was pretty worked up.

The small humans were just a few steps away from the picnic table when the big female called after them.

"Don't forget the rackets!" she yelled. "You need the rackets to hit the birdies!"

Poo-Poo, Mutt, and Karen all bared their teeth at this prospect as they watched the girl and boy grab two long-handled rackets from the picnic table bench.

"That's terrible!" Stripes cried, again speaking for the others. "Do they use the rackets as some kind of mega-weapons? Is that what's going on?!"

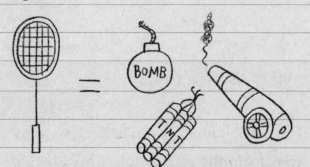

Stick Dog said nothing. He suspected that there was probably a more logical explanation. He didn't know what it was, but he suspected that "hitting birdies" might turn out to be like "hitting a dog with a stick"—it wasn't what it actually sounded like.

Mutt, Karen, and Stripes, however, had not considered that possibility at all. Their minds raced—and they were eager to share their ideas.

Poo-Poo, however, had already come up with a theory.

"They obviously use the rackets as wings," he said. "They flap them around super-duper fast. They rise into the air and chase the birdies that way. That's how they get them."

Karen, Mutt, and Stripes considered and
accepted Poo-Poo's theory.

Stick Dog did not.

To be honest, he had not been paying much
attention to the discussion. The boy and
girl had hustled off around the corner of
the house to the side yard. They were out
of sight. But Stick Dog now paid particular
attention to the older humans—the mother
and father.

The mom walked in and out of the house,
carrying something different each time.
The dad waited outside and took things
from her. Soon, he had spread a tablecloth,
arranged four plastic cups, and placed forks,
spoons, and knives around the table.

The mother came back a minute later with

a bowl. Its top was covered in aluminum foil. She said, "Here's the guacamole."

"What's left?" the father asked as he took the bowl and set it in the center.

"Let's see," the mother said, and pondered. As she did, the dad snuck his finger under the edge of the aluminum foil that covered the bowl. She listed everything for the meal. "Guacamole. Still need to get the chips. Tacos will be delivered soon. And the piñata at the end, of course."

Stick Dog watched and listened. He was surprised when the large male human withdrew his finger and there was a big glob of something green and chunky on it. He was even more surprised at what the man did next.

He licked the green
substance off his finger.

He said, "That's really good guacamole!"

"Don't do that!" the mother said. She
didn't seem mad at all. It was more like she
was kidding around. "We have to wait for
the tacos."

"When do they get here?" he asked, and
pressed the foil back down against the
bowl's rim.

"Shouldn't be too long,"
she answered. "I ordered
from Las Asadas on
Western. They make the
most delicious tacos in town."

"Excellent," he said. "Let's go get the game

started then. We'll show those kiddos a thing or two."

Stick Dog tried to put it all together as the humans left to play their game. He had never heard of "guacamole," "tacos," or "piñata" before. But he had some clues to work with. The big male human had eaten the "guacamole" and smiled. It had to be food—tasty food. He knew chips were food, of course. He'd had plenty of those over the years. The female human had said "tacos" were delicious. That meant they were food too. He now knew the unicorn in the tree was called a "piñata." The large humans had told the small humans to stop hitting the piñata. He didn't understand how that could be food at all.

"You guys," Stick Dog said after contemplating all of this information for several seconds. "I think—"

But he didn't get the chance to finish his thought.

His friends were way too worked up about something else. They had not been paying attention to the humans on the patio at all.

"Stick Dog," Poo-Poo interrupted. He had something rather urgent to say. "We've figured out the whole 'birdie' mystery. The little humans are going to flap the rackets like wings, fly into the air, and attack the birdies that way. Isn't that terrible?!"

"Hmm," Stick Dog replied, and paused. You could tell he didn't quite believe this particular theory. "I was going to say that I think—"

"Wait, wait," Stripes interjected. "I don't think you heard what Poo-Poo just said, Stick Dog. Those little humans are about to flap their racket-wings and fly all over the place in a mad birdie-attacking rampage. We have to stop them!"

"Umm, okay," replied Stick Dog hesitantly. "It's just I know that we're all hungry and I was listening to those big humans just now. And they just left. And I think I found—"

"Rampage, Stick Dog!" Mutt repeated urgently. "Birdie-attacking rampage!"

"Umm, but—"

"We have to stop it, Stick Dog!" Karen
pleaded. "We have to stop the rampage!
Just like we stopped the humans from
whacking that poor defenseless dog in the
tree. We have to go on another animal
rescue mission!"

"But that dog is really just a toy unicorn
hanging from that tree," Stick Dog
reminded them. For proof, he pointed at it.
"And we didn't rescue it. We didn't have to.
It's not alive. Look! It's still right there."

"Dog, unicorn, whatever!" Poo-Poo said.
He hopped up and down. He really wanted
to get moving. "Unicorn rescue, no unicorn
rescue! Whatever! We have to go! We have
to save the birdies!"

Mutt, Karen, and Stripes picked up on this idea and this refrain. They began to chant along with Poo-Poo.

"Save the birdies! Save the birdies!! Save the birdies!!!"

Stick Dog understood that it was no use. The guacamole—whatever that was—would have to wait.

"Okay, okay," he said. "The humans went around the side of the house. Let's go see what's going on."

And with that, the dogs stepped quietly from the woods and stalked across the backyard to the corner of the house.

What they saw when they got there confirmed Stick Dog's suspicion.

CHAPTER 8

TWANG!

All four humans were, indeed, there. However, they weren't—believe it or not—using their rackets as makeshift wings and flying about in the air to attack little birds all over the place.

You probably know what they were doing already, don't you?

They were playing badminton.

As if on cue, the boy screamed, "Hit the birdie to me!"

Stick Dog was completely grateful that the whole "Save the birdies" mission was now over and they could return to the strange, thick, green substance called guacamole on the picnic table. He had grown more and more curious about it as the minutes passed. And he had become more and more convinced that it might be something totally delicious.

"Come on, you guys," he said to his friends. He ducked behind the house corner again. His friends backed out of sight too. Stick Dog began to salivate. "We can go get that guacamole now. No rescue mission needed."

At this suggestion, Mutt, Poo-Poo, Stripes, and Karen all turned their heads to Stick Dog. Mutt asked a question on behalf of the group.

"What do you mean, Stick Dog?"

"There's no rescue mission," Stick Dog replied, and motioned toward the humans playing badminton. "Those humans are just batting that white floaty thing back and forth over that net. I think it must be called a 'birdie.' It's obviously not alive. And they're certainly not using the rackets for wings."

"That white floaty thing could be alive," Stripes said. The others didn't seem completely convinced either.

"Alive?" Stick Dog asked. He had a bad feeling about this—he realized it might take a little longer than he originally thought.

"Do you all think that motionless, wingless, beakless, silent, featherless plastic object is a bird? And not, you know, just a white thing that the humans hit around and just happen to call a birdie?"

"Sounds even more plausible and likely when you add it all up like that," Stripes said. She and the others had come to a very different conclusion than Stick Dog.

Now, this might have gone on for a while.

But it didn't.

That's because right then, the dad made an announcement.

"Okay," he said loudly. "One more warm-up rally. And then we start the game."

He dropped the birdie down to his racket
and hit it lazily across the net toward the
small female human.

The girl yelled, "Watch this!"

She pulled her racket way back as the
birdie fluttered and floated in a slow, gentle
descent from the top of its arc. As it drifted
closer and closer to her, the girl swung
the badminton racket forward with all her
physical power.

She grunted.

The birdie hit the racket in the exact center
of the strings.

TWANG!

TWANG!

The birdie rocketed from her racket and soared with great initial speed high up into the air. It was just beginning to slow down and descend when it stopped.

In a tree.

As Stick Dog observed all this, Stripes came up closer to him. She said, "Told you, Stick Dog."

"Told me what?"

"That white floaty thing *is* a little live birdie."

"I don't think so, Stripes," Stick Dog replied.

"Of course it is," Stripes declared with

confidence. "It just *flew* into the air and is now *perched* in that tree!"

Poo-Poo said, "That's what birds do, Stick Dog."

Karen added, "That proves it all right."

Mutt nodded his agreement as well.

Stick Dog had an important decision to make. He could debate the "Is it a real bird?" some more with his friends or he could try to devise a way to get them some of that thick, green, chunky stuff from the picnic table.

It was an easy decision to make.

Super-easy.

That's because right then Stick Dog's stomach grumbled in anticipation of a possible food discovery.

He said, "You guys are right. It *is* a birdie. I don't know what I was thinking."

"It sure takes you a long time to figure things out, Stick Dog," Karen said.

Stick Dog smiled, nodded in acknowledgment, and moved on.

He wasn't upset at all. That's because right at that moment the humans did something— and then the dogs got to eat something.

CHAPTER 9

GUAC-A-WHAT-EEE?

"Lizzy!" yelled the boy.

The girl started laughing. Her name must be Lizzy, Stick Dog figured.

"How are we going to get it down?" the boy asked. He didn't seem mad at all. He thought it was funny too.

"I had no idea how powerful I am!" Lizzy exclaimed, flexed her left bicep, and laughed some more.

"It's no big deal," the dad said. "Jacob, climb up on my shoulders. We might be able to reach it."

Stick Dog couldn't believe it. They didn't need a complicated strategy. They didn't need a perfectly executed plan.

No.

Stick Dog knew this: good timing often worked just as well as a good plan.

"They're going to be busy here for a while," he whispered to his friends. "We can go get some food now!"

"What?!" yelled Poo-Poo and Karen.

"Where?!" yelped Mutt and Stripes.

"I *think* it's food anyway," Stick Dog said. "It's thick and green. It's in a bowl on the picnic table on the patio. It's called guacamole. I heard the humans say it earlier."

"Guac-a-what-eee?" asked Poo-Poo. He and the others had never heard such a strange word before.

"Guac-a-mole-eee," Stick Dog pronounced slowly and phonetically. He yanked his head sideways toward the patio to try to get them to move. "That way."

His encouragement didn't work.

They didn't move.

"Is it made out of moles?" asked Stripes suspiciously. "If so, I don't want any.  Moles are gross. All that scurrying around and digging and stuff. And their weird pink noses! No thank you."

"I doubt if it's made out of moles," Stick Dog answered quickly. He didn't want the conversation to veer off into a time-consuming exchange about moles. "It's green—and moles are not green."

"Maybe it's made out of guacs," suggested Karen.

Stick Dog couldn't help himself, he had to ask. "What are 'guacs'? Have you ever heard that word before, Karen?"

"Sure I have," answered Karen confidently. "It's a big group of birds."

"That's a 'flock,'" Stick Dog said, but his friends didn't seem to notice. They were intrigued by Karen's bird idea.

"So that thick green stuff is made out of birds, hunh?" Mutt asked, and nodded his head. "Might be tasty then. I've had chicken and turkey before. You know, on a sandwich or something I've found at Picasso Park or on the school playground."

"It's not made out of—" Stick Dog said, but he couldn't complete his thought.

"This new food is green," Poo-Poo interrupted, joining in. "So it must be made out of *green* birds. Parrots, finches, pterodactyls, hummingbirds, parakeets. Those kinds of birds. See, I think the humans catch a bunch of those green birds. Maybe they put them in a cage and listen to their beautiful songs for a while. They probably fatten them up by feeding them a bunch of worms and seeds and stuff. And when they get nice and plump, they pop those cute little green birds into a pot and boil them. Then they mash them all up into this guacamole dish. It's all perfectly clear now."

Stripes, Mutt, and Karen all seemed to think that Poo-Poo made a lot of sense.

Stick Dog took a moment to himself then. He lowered his head, closed his eyes, and tried to think of calm, soothing things. He thought of the way the leaves in the trees rustle when there's a gentle autumn breeze. He thought of the slow-moving water in the creek as it sloshes and babbles along.

After this brief meditation, Stick Dog raised his head and calmly said, "I'm certain it's not made out of green birds. I don't know what it *is* actually made of, but I can tell you something for sure."

Mutt asked, "What's that, Stick Dog?"

"I saw the big male human dip his finger into that bowl on the picnic table. The one with the silver paper on top," Stick Dog replied. "That's the one the guacamole is in. When he pulled his finger out, he licked the green guacamole off. It looked like he really enjoyed the way it tasted!"

Well, that's all Stripes, Mutt, Karen, and Poo-Poo needed to hear. Poo-Poo asked the question that was on all their minds.

He asked, "How do we get it?"

"What do you mean?" replied Stick Dog.

Poo-Poo asked, "What's the plan?"

"There's no plan," Stick Dog said. He was a little dumbfounded, but he decided to simply state the obvious. "The humans are all *that* way. And the guacamole is over *this* way. We just, you know, go get it."

With that good news, Poo-Poo, Mutt, Stripes, and Karen happily followed Stick Dog as he scampered toward the patio. As he did, Stick Dog's confidence grew. That's because he could hear the four humans talking from the side yard. As long as he could hear them, he was fairly sure he could deduce if they were coming back. He stopped about halfway across the yard to listen to their conversation. The others stopped with him.

"Nope. Can't reach it from here," the dad said. "Lizzy, hand a racket up to Jake. Maybe we can reach it that way. Mom, you make sure he doesn't fall off."

Stick Dog turned to his friends and smiled. "We've got some time."

They hustled the rest of the way to the patio. When they got there, Stick Dog eyed that bowl of guacamole on the picnic table.

He took one step toward it.

He reached toward it.

And then stopped.

They weren't going to get that guacamole.

Not yet.

CHAPTER 10

THERE'S A DOG IN THE BOWL

A car horn honked from the front of the house.

HONK!

And Stick Dog heard what the mom said next.

"That must be the taco man from Las Asadas," she said loudly. "I'll be right back."

"Shoot," Stick Dog said. There was disappointment in his voice.

"What's the matter?" asked Mutt.

"The big female human is coming back," Stick Dog said, and turned around to race back to the safety and cover of the forest. "We have to leave! Now!"

By the time all the dogs dove and tumbled into the woods, the mom had bought and paid for a big sack of tacos from the delivery man.

LAS
ASADAS
TACOS

Stick Dog stared at the back door as he crouched behind the branches and brambles of a blackberry bush. And in just a moment, the mom came out holding that sack. She placed it on the picnic table next to the guacamole bowl.

"Sorry, you guys. I don't think we can get

that guacamole," Stick Dog said. "I think they're going to be eating soon."

"What's guacamole again?" asked Karen. She, Mutt, Stripes, and Poo-Poo all watched from beneath a huge pine tree. It was shady and cool there. Several big brown pinecones were scattered about on the ground.

"It's in the bowl with the shiny silver covering," answered Stick Dog. He pointed toward the picnic table. "It's green—"

He was interrupted by Stripes.

"It's made out of cooked green birds," she reminded Karen wrongly. "Remember?"

"Oh, right."

Stick Dog decided not to correct Stripes and

instead turned back toward the patio. The mom did just what the dad did earlier. She lifted the edge of the aluminum foil, dipped her forefinger into the bowl, and licked a big dollop of guacamole from it. She kept looking toward the corner of the house to ensure that nobody from her family was coming. She dipped her finger a second and third time—and with each lick she smiled a satisfied smile.

"That's what guacamole is," Stick Dog said. "She's eating some right now."

"She likes it," observed Poo-Poo. "She really likes it."

"What's she doing now, Stick Dog?" asked Mutt.

"I don't know. Let's watch."

The woman moved away from the guacamole bowl and began searching for something else on the table.

"The chips. Where are the chips?" the mom asked, and snapped her fingers. Then she called out loudly enough for the rest of her family to hear. "Did you guys remember to pick up tortilla chips at the store?"

The dad answered from around the corner of the house. "Yes," he called. "They're in one of the bags in the kitchen."

"Okay. I'll get them," the mom answered.

"Any luck getting the birdie out of the tree?"

"Still working on it!"

The mom nodded and smiled. She went back inside the house.

"Are you kidding me?" Stick Dog said.

"What?" asked Poo-Poo.

"She's leaving. I can't believe it," he answered. Stick Dog was genuinely surprised. "The big female went inside again. The rest of the family is trying to get that birdie out of the tree. They're all gone!"

"What's so great about that?" asked Stripes.

"They're all gone!" repeated Stick Dog.

"What's your point?" asked Mutt.

Stick Dog pointed to the patio where there were, you know, no humans at all. He said, "Gone!"

Poo-Poo said, "You need to explain yourself more clearly, Stick Dog."

"Yeah," Karen added. "We can't read your mind, you know."

"Umm," said Stick Dog slowly. Then he picked up the pace of his speech a lot. Stick Dog knew the mom would likely only be inside for a moment or two. It didn't take long to retrieve a bag of chips, after all. But Stick Dog also knew this: he and his friends were fast. They could run fast—and they could eat even faster. He thought there might be—there just might be—enough time to get that guacamole. But they needed to get moving. Right now. He said, "It means we can go get that guacamole and not get caught!"

"Why didn't you just say so?" asked Poo-Poo as they hurtled out of the woods and sprinted across the backyard to the patio.

Stripes got there first. She was the fastest.

With her back legs on the bench, Stripes propped herself up to the table. She clenched a loose edge of the shiny

aluminum foil and began to lift it from the
bowl with her mouth.

But she paused.

She began to shiver. She held perfectly
still—except for her own slight trembling.
The aluminum foil rattled and clattered a bit.

"What's wrong, Stripes?" Stick Dog asked
quickly. He could tell she was startled—
even frightened—by something.

"There's a d-dog in the b-bowl."

"What?"

"Th-th-there's a d-dog in the b-bowl,"
Stripes whispered. "It's staring r-right up at
m-me."

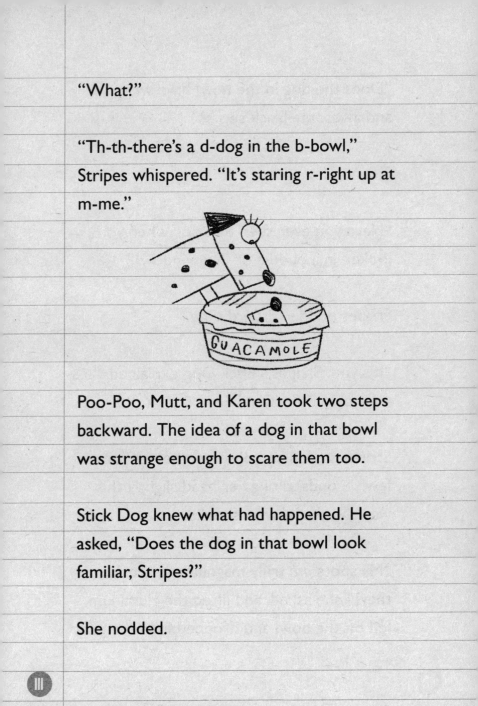

Poo-Poo, Mutt, and Karen took two steps
backward. The idea of a dog in that bowl
was strange enough to scare them too.

Stick Dog knew what had happened. He
asked, "Does the dog in that bowl look
familiar, Stripes?"

She nodded.

"Does the dog in the bowl have white fur and awesome black spots?"

She nodded again.

"Have you ever seen that dog when you looked in a puddle or in a window?"

Stripes nodded a third time.

"It's you, Stripes," Stick Dog explained. "It's your own reflection."

Stripes smiled and observed herself for a few seconds, tilting her head slightly this way and that way as she did.

"My spots *are* truly magnificent, aren't they?" she asked, and lifted the aluminum foil off the bowl and dropped it to the patio.

The bowl was full of thick, chunky, green guacamole.

There was no hesitation.

All five dogs dipped their paws into the bowl one time. And each of them got a great green clump of the food on their paw pads.

Stick Dog licked his paw quickly.

The guacamole was delicious.

Super-delicious.

"Get some more as fast as you can!" Stick Dog urged his companions. "We don't have much time!"

With that message delivered, Stick Dog hurried to an open window at the back of the house, propped himself up on the sill, and peeked inside. The big female human was digging through grocery bags in the kitchen. She hadn't found the chips yet.

Stick Dog knew they might have one more minute.

At the most.

As he raced to his friends, he could see Karen, Stripes, and Mutt turn to Poo-Poo. Stick Dog knew exactly what was happening. Whenever they discovered something new to eat, Poo-Poo provided an expert analysis.

"You'll be happy to hear that this so-called 'guacamole' has no moles in it at all," Poo-Poo began. His head was elevated slightly above the others. His eyelids were one-quarter closed. He spoke in a clear, authoritative tone. "And no green birds either. No parakeets or finches here. No, indeed. Rather, this chunky green goo seems to be entirely vegetable-based. I taste hints of onion and cilantro, but it's the texture that truly defines the dish. There's a creaminess here that pulls the whole thing together. It spreads evenly in my mouth and then lingers longer because of it. It's this texture that really lifts this newfangled food from pedestrian sustenance to culinary delight."

CULINARY DELIGHT.

Mutt, Stripes, and Karen tilted their heads and stared at Poo-Poo then. They didn't quite understand everything he had just said. The truth was they weren't even sure if Poo-Poo himself understood what he had just said.

Karen asked, "You mean it tastes good?"

"It tastes great!" replied Poo-Poo. With that confirmation, all four dogs plunged their paws into the bowl for another helping.

Half the guacamole was gone when Stick Dog got back to his friends. He was just about to reach his paw in for a second taste.

But he never got it.

Right then he heard the big female human inside the house. Her voice carried out of the open kitchen window.

"There they are!" the mom exclaimed inside the house. "In the very last bag, of course."

"She found the chips," Stick Dog whispered to himself. And then to his friends, he said, "Back to the forest!"

BACK TO THE FOREST!

CHAPTER 11

CHEW-CRUNCH-CHEW

Stick Dog watched the
female human return to
the patio. She carried a
large cellophane bag in
her hand.

Stick Dog whispered, "That must be the
chips."

"What a massive disappointment," Karen
commented as she and the others peered
out from the edge of the woods.

"What's the matter, Karen?" asked Mutt.

"Didn't you like the guacamole?"

"No, that's not it," Karen replied, and licked some of the remaining green goop from her lips. "It was quite good. It's just that I thought she might be coming back with barbecue potato chips. And those don't look like barbecue potato chips at all."

The mom had torn the bag open, set it down on the table, and pulled a couple of chips out.

"How do you know they're not barbecue potato chips?" asked Stripes. "Maybe they are."

"They're not," Karen said, and shook her head. "Barbecue potato chips are a different color. And they're all different shapes and sizes too. They're kind of circular. They have curves and bends and wrinkles. Oh, and sometimes they're folded over on themselves. Those foldy ones are the best! The absolute best!"

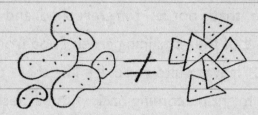

"Are you sure they aren't barbecue potato chips?" asked Poo-Poo.

"Positive. Those chips are triangles. And they're thick," Karen pointed out. She seemed disappointed. "And none of them are folded."

Stick Dog focused on the chip in the big female's hand. Karen was right: it was shaped like a triangle. And it did look thicker than the potato chips they had often found in the past.

The mom took two steps toward the bowl.

She eyed the aluminum foil for a couple
of seconds, then shrugged and started to
remove it.

Panic coursed instantly through Stick Dog's
body. And questions raced through his mind.

Had she noticed something peculiar or out
of place about the shiny sheet covering
the bowl? Could she tell the foil had been
removed and replaced? Would there be too
much guacamole missing? Would she see
paw prints in the guacamole itself? Would
this be the end of their mission?

Stick Dog certainly hoped not. He wanted
some more guacamole for his friends—and
for himself.

And he wanted to find out more about the
"tacos" that were mentioned earlier. He had

never heard that word before—but it intrigued
him. He was pretty sure tacos
could be food too. He had been
so focused on the guacamole
and keeping his friends safe that
Stick Dog hadn't even examined
the bag full of tacos.

He watched nervously as the big female
human's fingertips gripped the edge of the
foil and lifted it from the bowl.

Stick Dog watched.

And waited.

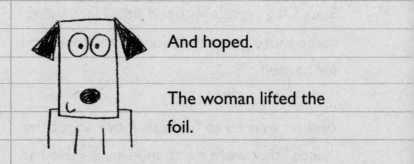

And hoped.

The woman lifted the
foil.

And then a voice came calling from the side of the house.

"Mom!" It was the smaller human boy's voice.

MOM!

The woman snapped her head around and toward the sound. As she did, she dipped one corner of that triangular chip blindly into the bowl and pulled it out with a great green clump of guacamole on it.

"What?" she called back. Then she shoved the loaded chip into her mouth.

"We can't get the birdie out of the tree!"

After taking a few seconds to chew and swallow, the mom yelled, "Coming!"

She then pushed the foil back onto the bowl so quickly that she didn't even notice how much guacamole was missing. And she certainly didn't have time to see the strange paw-shaped indentations in the guacamole itself.

"I can't believe it," Stick Dog whispered as he watched the big female human leave again.

"Me neither," said Poo-Poo. He seemed surprised by something too. "You can't combine foods that way. It's totally bizarre."

"That's not what I mean," Stick Dog said. "I can't believe we have another chance to—"

"Why's it so bizarre?" Karen asked Poo-Poo,

not realizing that she interrupted Stick Dog.

"Every food should be enjoyed on its own merits, that's why," Poo-Poo answered authoritatively. He had earned his reputation as the leading food critic in the group and was all too happy to share his opinions. "Combining the guacamole with that weird triangle chip just doesn't make sense."

"Why not, Poo-Poo?" asked Mutt.

"Guys, we should probably—" Stick Dog tried to interject, but Poo-Poo was already answering Mutt's inquiry in a proud, loud, and absolute voice.

"Food is meant to be enjoyed one flavor at a time, that's why not," Poo-Poo declared.

"Well, I don't know about that," Mutt said.

He wasn't totally convinced. "Sometimes, when I shake something from my fur to eat, more than one thing pops out. Just yesterday I was feeling a little snack-ish— you know just needed something to chew on for a bit. So, I shook. And out popped half a mitten and a plastic water bottle."

"What happened then, Mutt?" asked Stripes.

"We're running out of—" Stick Dog tried to interject again, but nobody paid any attention to him at all.

"Well," Mutt continued, "I realized that the soft, chewy texture of the mitten and the hard, crunchy traits of the bottle combined nicely. I went back and forth between the two items quite often. It was sort of like this: *Crunch-crunch-chew. Chew-chew-crunch.* And sometimes, when I felt really adventurous, it was more like this: *Crunch-chew-crunch* or *chew-crunch-chew.* I found the experience both lovely and satisfying."

"That makes total sense," said Karen.

Stripes agreed.

But Poo-Poo did not. He didn't like to have his role as food expert questioned.

"Textures are not flavors," he insisted. "That's like comparing apples and oranges."

"I bet those are good together," said Mutt, sticking to his point.

Stick Dog had been as patient as he could be. He stepped closer to his friends and raised his physical stature a bit. He lifted his shoulders a little higher.

"It's a very interesting discussion," he said as soon as he got the chance. "And I have a great way to investigate it further."

"How's that?" asked Poo-Poo.

"Let's try those triangle chips and guacamole together ourselves. Let's dip the chips just like the human did," Stick Dog suggested quickly. He calculated that the mom had likely arrived to join the rest of her family by now. They were bound to get that birdie out of the tree soon. Stick Dog knew there wasn't much time left. "If you like the combination of flavors, you can continue to eat both things together. If you don't, you can eat them separately."

This seemed to satisfy everybody.

And Stick Dog said just one thing.

One simple thing.

"Let's go!"

CHAPTER 12

THAT MUST BE A TACO

They got back to the picnic table in seventeen seconds. Stripes lifted the shiny foil from the guacamole bowl while Stick Dog lifted the bag of triangular chips off the table. He tipped it until a bunch of chips fell out to the ground.

"Okay," Stick Dog instructed as fast as he could. "Here are the chips! Dip them in and see what it's like. I'm going to take a quick look around the corner of the house."

He booked to that corner, skidded to a stop, and peeked around the edge. He could

see the entire family of
four standing beneath the
tree. They stared up at
that birdie. The mom and
dad had their hands on
their hips.

The birdie was still stuck.

They had a little more time.

Stick Dog hurried back to his friends. He
was anxious to see if they were enjoying the
chips and guacamole. When he arrived at
the picnic table several seconds later, Stick
Dog was shocked at what he saw.

Poo-Poo, Stripes, Mutt, and Karen had
not even tasted the guacamole-and-chips
combination yet. They each had a chip in

their mouth—and each chip had a dollop of the chunky green goop on it. But they were not eating.

"What's the matter?" asked Stick Dog. "Why aren't you guys eating?"

Mutt answered for the whole group. They were each, obviously, in the same predicament.

"We can't—figure—it out," Mutt began to explain. With that chip dangling from one corner of his mouth, he could only get one or two words out at a time. If his mouth was open too long, the chip would fall out.

"So you each grabbed a chip with your mouths and dipped it in the bowl?" Stick Dog asked, and smiled. "But you can't get it the rest of the way into your mouths?"

They all nodded.

"Try this," suggested Stick Dog. "Lift your chins up quickly and let go of the chip. It will shoot up into the air a bit, hover a little, and you can then snatch the whole thing in your mouths."

This idea made absolute sense to them all. And they immediately flipped their chips up in the air a few inches, caught them—and ate them.

Now, not only did the dogs discover that chips and guacamole were delicious together, they also found this new eating technique a lot of fun.

They dipped and tossed and flipped and caught and chewed and swallowed for the next two minutes.

Stick Dog listened as he ate three guacamole-dipped chips. Then he checked around the house corner again. Now the mom was on the dad's shoulders. She had one of the rackets in her hand and swiped up at the birdie.

She couldn't reach it.

"We need something longer," the dad said, and lowered her down from his shoulders. He clapped his hands and said, "I know what we can use! The umbrella. I'll go get it."

"No more time," Stick Dog whispered to himself, and jerked his head back.

He pivoted in place and ran as fast as he could back to the table. By the time Stick Dog got there, the guacamole was all gone and there were just a few chips left on the ground.

Karen had her whole head in the bowl, licking the final guacamole remnants from its sides.

"Back to the woods!" Stick Dog urged when he got there. He nudged Karen's left hip with his nose to ensure that she had heard him. "The big male human is coming back!"

Karen backed out of the bowl, saw that Mutt, Poo-Poo, and Stripes were already hustling toward the tree line, and darted after them.

Stick Dog pressed the loose sheet of tin foil onto the bowl again and zoomed across the yard.

The man arrived back at the patio at the precise moment Stick Dog settled into a secure hiding place.

Stick Dog watched and studied the man from that safe distance. He was acting strange. He said he was doing things that he wasn't actually doing.

"I'll be right there," the man called to his family. He hadn't even noticed the spilled chips. His mind—and his appetite—were focused on something else entirely. He reached into the taco bag and pulled out a hand-sized cylindrical object. It was wrapped in the same kind of aluminum foil that covered the guacamole bowl. "Just getting the umbrella."

Then the dad did a most unusual thing. He said something else. He whispered it. His family couldn't hear it.

But Stick Dog could hear it.

Dogs, you know, can hear way better than humans.

 The man whispered, "Oh, I'll get the umbrella. But first I'm going to have a carne asada taco."

"That must be a taco," Stick Dog said, and watched.

The man unwrapped the foil from the taco right when a soft summer breeze swooshed across the back patio on its way to the woods. It carried the scent of that steak taco across the lawn—and toward the dogs.

All five dogs smelled its juicy, meaty goodness on the breeze.

"Stick Dog?" Poo-Poo said.

"Yes?"

"We *REALLY* want to get those tacos."

Stick Dog nodded but didn't say anything. His eyes never left that large male human. He watched him tilt the taco and his head sideways so the contents wouldn't fall out. He watched him take his first big bite. Then the man yelled to his family.

"Be there in a minute!"

He took a second bite and yelled again.

"Having a little trouble with the umbrella!"

He took a third bite.

"There, I got it!"

He took a fourth bite.

"On my way!"

He took a fifth and final bite, chewed, and swallowed. He then lifted the umbrella easily from its stand, folded it shut, and headed back to his family. He smiled to himself and licked his lips.

Stick Dog stared at the large male human as he exited the scene. The patio was empty. There were no humans anywhere. The taco bag stood there on that picnic table unguarded.

But he didn't lead his friends to that bag.

Not yet.

Something else had caught his eye.

A second summer breeze had blown across the backyard. The unicorn hanging from the tree swayed a bit. Stick Dog's eyes narrowed.

"What are we waiting for?!" Stripes exclaimed. "Let's go!"

She, Mutt, Karen, and Poo-Poo had all edged almost completely out of the woods.

"Wait," Stick Dog said calmly. He looked all around their surroundings. And he saw something that just might work. "Mutt, can you come here, please?"

Mutt came closer.

"Do you mind if I put some things in your fur?"

"Not at all, Stick Dog," Mutt said graciously. "My shaggy locks are completely at your disposal."

"Thank you."

With that, Stick Dog quickly and gently shoved several of the pinecones scattered about on the forest floor into Mutt's fur. It took less than a minute.

And when that short task was done, Stick Dog turned to his friends who were all drooling at the edge of the woods. He said, "It's taco time."

CHAPTER 13

TACO TIME

It took less than twelve seconds for the dogs to cross that backyard. And there was absolutely no hesitation when they got there. Stick Dog propped himself up to the table, reached for the bag of tacos, and pulled it down. He dumped all the tacos onto the patio.

There were nine tacos. Each one was wrapped tightly in aluminum foil.

Mutt, Karen, Stripes, and Poo-Poo stood
in a circle around the tacos. They stared
down at them. They drooled over them. It
looked like they could barely believe this was
actually happening.

Stick Dog smiled and said, "Each of you
eat one for now. When you unwrap them,
try not to tear that shiny silver cover too
much."

"Aren't you going to have a taco, Stick Dog?"
asked Mutt.

"I am, hopefully," he answered. "I need to
check on the humans first."

And that's just what Stick Dog did.

As his friends unwrapped and devoured their
tacos, Stick Dog hurried off toward the side

yard again. He edged his muzzle inch by inch around the corner of the house until he could see the humans.

They didn't spot him at all. Their backs were to him—and they stared up into that tree where the birdie was still stuck. The large male human poked the umbrella way up into the tree. Stick Dog could tell that this time they would reach the birdie—and get it down.

Stick Dog hustled back.

Each of his friends was about halfway done eating their first taco. They didn't need to worry about tipping the taco sideways like the dad earlier. Any taco contents that fell out, they just ate off the patio anyway. No big deal.

Stick Dog asked, "Mutt, do you mind if I retrieve some of those pinecones I put in your fur?"

Mutt swallowed politely before answering. He didn't want to be rude and answer while he was chewing. He also didn't want to let a single morsel of that taco goodness fall from his mouth.

"Help yourself, Stick Dog," Mutt replied. "Help yourself."

"Thanks,"
Stick Dog
said, and

started to pull pinecones from Mutt's shaggy fur.

While Poo-Poo, Karen, Mutt, and Stripes finished their tacos, Stick Dog did something entirely different.

He took the four pieces of loose aluminum foil and wrapped up a pinecone with each piece. He then unwrapped the five remaining tacos and did the same thing with them, leaving the tacos themselves on the patio for the time being.

As fast as he could, Stick Dog placed the nine aluminum-foil-wrapped pinecones in the taco bag and lifted it back up to the picnic table. Right when he did, he heard all four members of the human family yell happily from the side yard.

"They got the birdie down," Stick Dog whispered to himself. He yanked his head over his shoulder and said to his friends, "Grab a second taco each. Take it to the woods! Now!"

They did exactly as he instructed. Stick Dog himself took his first taco in his mouth and raced after his friends.

They reached the safety of the woods just as the dad turned the corner of the house with the umbrella under his arm.

CHAPTER 14

BUSTED. ALMOST.

The dad returned the umbrella to the patio, propping it up in its stand and lifting its bright orange canopy until it locked into place.

As he did, Mutt, Karen, Poo-Poo, and Stripes enjoyed their second tacos in the shade of that big pine tree.

And as his friends enjoyed their second tacos, Stick Dog ate his first. He was well hidden but still in the sunshine. It was delicious— and Stick Dog savored those flavors in his mouth, chewing slowly. As he chewed, he kept an eye on that large male human.

After successfully returning the umbrella, the dad looked cautiously toward the corner of the house. It seemed like he didn't want to get caught doing something—again. He shoved his right hand into that bag and pulled out another taco.

Only it wasn't a taco.

It was a pinecone.

Stick Dog knew it.

But the large male human did not know it.

Yet.

Stick Dog stopped chewing and watched.
If the large male human found the pinecone,
Stick Dog would lead his friends back
through the woods—and back to the safety
of his pipe under Highway 16. They were
fed for the night. If they had to leave now,
it would be okay. They had, after all,
enjoyed guacamole, chips, and tacos.

But Stick Dog wanted a little more time—
just a little more time—to do one more
thing here. He wasn't quite sure what it
was, but his instincts told him there was
more to accomplish.

Unfortunately, Stick Dog was not going to
get the chance. The large male human began

to peel the first bit of aluminum foil off that pinecone that he thought was a taco.

Stick Dog knew this food-finding mission was over.

The human unwrapped the aluminum foil a bit more.

Stick Dog turned to his friends. It was time to tell them to hurry back to his pipe.

But Stick Dog didn't tell them that at all.

Right then, the small female human called from the other side of the house.

"Dad! Come on!" she screamed. "Let's play the game so we can get to dinner!"

DAD!

The large male human stopped and held still. He looked down at the taco in his hand and then to the corner of the house. He looked back and forth two more times.

And then he pressed the aluminum foil back in place.

"Coming!" he called, and shoved the pinecone back into the bag and began to walk toward the side yard. "One game to twenty-one points! Parents versus kids. Then dinner!"

CHAPTER 15

MORE TO DO

As the big male human turned the corner of the house, Stick Dog felt a comforting sense of satisfaction. He had led his friends to two entirely new, filling, and scrumptious foods. The guacamole and tacos had not only introduced them to unique and delectable flavors—the new foods had also filled their hungry bellies.

His friends were happy and fed.

Stick Dog himself was happy and fed.

But there was still one thing that nagged at him from the corner of his mind.

That unicorn.

That gosh-darned unicorn.

He had questions about it—bothersome questions that left his mind unsettled. He had a feeling there was still more to achieve on this food-finding quest.

"Can I ask you all a couple of questions?" asked Stick Dog. He was situated in the bright sunshine outside that pine tree's circle of shade.

"Of course," Mutt answered for them all

as he, Poo-Poo, Stripes, and Karen plopped down in the shade to relax.

"Why do you think the humans hung that unicorn up in that tree? And why were the little humans hitting it with a stick when we got here?"

As they relaxed, the dogs contemplated Stick Dog's questions. After a moment, Poo-Poo responded.

"I think I know why they were hitting the unicorn, Stick Dog," he said.

"Okay. Why then?"

"It's fun to hit things, that's why," Poo-Poo answered succinctly. "And I should know. I hit my head into things all the time. It's a blast! Garbage cans. Parked cars. Trees.

Whatever. Yes, indeed, some hearty head-bashing is great fun. And hitting stuff with a stick must be fun too."

"I'm not so sure," said Stick Dog. "I think there might be more to it than that."

"They did seem to be enjoying themselves," Mutt said, backing up Poo-Poo's theory.

"That's true," Stick Dog admitted.

"And they were laughing," Stripes added.

Stick Dog nodded his head. That was true too.

"And they wanted to keep hitting it," Karen pitched in. "The big humans made them stop. They said to save it for after the guacamole and tacos."

Stick Dog nodded again and began to pace. Those small humans definitely did enjoy hitting the unicorn. But Stick Dog thought there was something here—a specific clue—that he just couldn't quite put his paw on.

Stick Dog took three more steps and jerked to a stop again.

He had it.

He figured it out.

Poo-Poo, Stripes, Mutt, and Karen were all too

familiar with the look that appeared on Stick Dog's face right then. They stood up from their relaxed positions and came closer to him.

"What is it, Stick Dog?" Karen asked for all of them. "What's going on?"

"The big humans wanted to save the unicorn until after they finished their meal," he explained as a sly smile built on his face. "Now, I have another question for you."

His friends had quickly regained their energy and enthusiasm. Karen shivered her long dachshund body from nose to tail. Stripes jumped up and down. Mutt gave his fur a vigorous, cleansing shake. And Poo-Poo hurried even closer to Stick Dog.

"What is it, Stick Dog?" he asked.

Stick Dog looked at his friends, making direct eye contact with each of them.

"My question is this," Stick Dog said. "What comes after a meal?"

Stripes, Poo-Poo, Karen, and Mutt all answered at the same time.

"Dessert!"

"That's exactly right!" Stick Dog said and smiled. "I think that unicorn is their dessert."

This did not make sense to his friends at all. Karen stopped shivering. Stripes stopped jumping. Mutt stopped shaking. And Poo-Poo tilted his head sideways and asked the question they were all wondering.

"Hunh?"

"The unicorn is dessert."

With doubt on his face and in his voice, Poo-Poo said, "It doesn't even look edible."

"It looks like it's made out of paper," Mutt added.

"Humans don't hang dessert in trees," Stripes added.

"I don't think you're supposed to eat unicorns anyway, Stick Dog," said Karen.

"I think they're special. Like magical. They need to be protected."

"Umm, it's not a real unicorn," Stick Dog replied to Karen. "Remember?"

Poo-Poo slowly placed his front left paw around Stick Dog's shoulder.

"Hey, buddy," Poo-Poo said in the best soothing voice he could muster.

"Yes?" Stick Dog answered slowly. He wasn't sure what Poo-Poo was about to say, but this tone of voice was certainly strange.

"Why don't you come out of the sun," Poo-Poo said in that super-soft voice. He gave Stick Dog a little nudge and added, "Let's get you into the shade."

"Why?" asked Stick Dog.

"Listen, old pal," Poo-Poo replied. "I think you've been out in the heat too long. I think the sun might have cooked your brain."

Stick Dog gently removed Poo-Poo's paw from his shoulder.

"I appreciate your concern," Stick Dog said, and smiled. Then he explained his theory further. "I think the dessert could be *inside* that unicorn. I think the little humans hit it with a stick to try to break it open. I think it's like a game-and-dessert combination."

"But how are we going to get it down?" asked Stripes.

"And how are we going to break it open?" asked Karen.

"I haven't figured that out yet," Stick Dog said, and cocked his head in the direction of the badminton game in the side yard. He wanted to hear the score. After several seconds, he did. The big male human called it out. It was 5–3. They were playing to twenty-one. Stick Dog said to his friends, "We still have some time—but not much. A few minutes. Let's go!"

And they went.

CHAPTER 16

STICK DOG, THE COWBOY

They sprinted across the backyard as fast as they could, skidding and tumbling to a stop beneath the slowly swaying unicorn.

The unicorn hung and swung from a single piece of thick twine. The twine was tied to a high branch and connected to a little loop on the unicorn's back.

Stripes—the best jumper in the group—began to spring into the air. She stretched and swiped at the unicorn when she reached the apex of her jump.

It wasn't even close.

Even with her awesome jumping ability, Stripes was still a good two or three feet short of reaching that unicorn.

"No way. I can't do it," Stripes concluded after her third attempt. "It's too high—even for me."

Stick Dog listened for the score of the humans' game.

It was 7–5.

7-5!

They still had some time.

He looked around on the patio for something—anything—they might be able to use to reach that unicorn.

The picnic table was too heavy to push across the patio and climb on. And there wasn't much on it to use, that was for sure. There were just the eating utensils, the ball of twine the humans must have used to tie the unicorn up in the first place, the empty guacamole bowl, and two bags—one with some tortilla chips left inside and one with nine wrapped-up pinecones disguised as tacos.

"There has to be some way to get up there," Stick Dog said. He was really just thinking out loud, but his words prompted a suggestion from Karen.

"We could act like beavers," Karen suggested. "You know, those toothy rascals we see at the creek sometimes? We could act like them."

"How so, Karen?" asked Mutt.

"We just all bite and gnaw at the tree trunk," Karen explained further. She bared her teeth for her friends to see before continuing. "Among my many unique traits are my super-sharp teeth. I'll take the lead, but you all can bite and munch on the tree trunk with me. Once we chew all the way through—*TIMBER!*—the tree and the unicorn crash to the ground. Simple stuff."

Mutt and Stripes nodded their heads. Poo-Poo exposed his sharp tree-biting incisors. They all seemed to like Karen's idea.

Stick Dog, still trying to come up with a more, umm, practical unicorn-snatching strategy, had overheard Karen's plan.

"It's a terrific plan, Karen," Stick Dog said sincerely—and quickly. "But the score of the humans' game is now eight to seven. It's going to be over really soon. I don't think we have time to, you know, chew through this massive tree trunk."

"Bummer," Karen said.

"How do you know the score of their strange birdie-smashing game, Stick Dog?" asked Mutt.

"I'm listening closely," answered Stick

Dog. "They're playing their game to twenty-one points. As soon as one team scores that much, the game's over. That's when we need to get out of here— before they get back and realize that the guacamole and tacos are missing."

To demonstrate, Stick Dog held still and lifted his left ear toward the corner of the house. The others listened too.

In a few seconds, the dad's voice came bellowing from the side yard.

"It's nine to eight," he yelled. "One more point and she's all tied up!"

9-8!

Now, there were two important things about what that dad yelled.

The first was obvious. With a score of 9–8, Stick Dog knew they were running out of time. Twenty-one was not too far away.

But Stick Dog already knew that. It was the second thing the big male human said that was even more important.

Do you know what it was?

I'll tell you.

After the dad called out the score, he said, "One more point and she's all tied up!"

Stick Dog snapped his head to the right and stared at Karen for a single second. He snapped his head to the left and stared at that ball of thick twine on the picnic table.

Stick Dog had a plan—and a determined look on his face.

Mutt, Stripes, Poo-Poo, and Karen didn't need to ask if Stick Dog had a plan to get the unicorn out of the tree.

They *knew* Stick Dog had a plan to get the unicorn out of the tree.

 "What do we do, Stick Dog?" Poo-Poo asked.

"The four of you get under the unicorn," he answered urgently as he jumped from the patio to the picnic table bench—and then to the top of the table.

Stick Dog did several things quickly.

1. He began to uncoil the thick twine from its roll.

2. He gave his friends further instructions, calling, "Gather around Karen!"

3. He listened for the score of the humans' game. He heard the big male human yell, "It's a close game! Eleven to ten!"

4. With a big pile of loose, thick string now, Stick Dog snatched the ball of twine in his mouth and scooted to the edge of the table.

While Stick Dog did all of these things, Mutt, Poo-Poo, and Stripes formed a misshapen circle around Karen and discussed it all.

"What do you think Stick Dog's plan is?" asked Poo-Poo.

"I think I know," said Stripes. She seemed pretty sure of herself. "You see how he got that string and unwrapped it?"

Mutt, Karen, and Poo-Poo confirmed this fact.

"Well, I think he's making a lasso," Stripes continued. "I think he's going to be a cowboy. As soon as that unicorn starts running away, he's going to hop on a horse, gallop after the unicorn, throw his lasso around its neck, and catch it."

"I've always wanted to ride a horse!" Karen exclaimed. "When do you think Stick Dog's horse will arrive? Maybe he'll let me ride it!"

"It should be any minute," Stripes affirmed. "We are a little pressed for time, after all."

As soon as Stripes mentioned this, she, Karen, Mutt, and Poo-Poo began jerking their heads around to look for an approaching horse. They looked toward the woods and to each side of the house. And, for some reason, Stripes looked high up into the topmost branches of the tree.

"Hey, Stick Dog!" Karen called.

"Yes?" he mumbled. The ball of twine was clenched in his mouth.

"Is it okay if I take a turn?" Karen yelled. She nodded really fast and smiled a lot. She was excited.

"A turn . . . at . . . what?" Stick Dog mumbled some more. He could only get a couple of syllables out at a time without dropping the ball of twine.

"A turn at riding the horse, of course!" Karen called.

"What . . . horse?"

"The one you ride when you're a cowboy!"

"What?"

"When you act like a cowboy and ride a horse and catch the unicorn with your handy-dandy lasso! That horse!"

Stick Dog instantly realized he was going to need more words—spoken quickly—to figure out what in heaven's name Karen was talking about. He dropped the twine at the edge of the table, ensured that it wouldn't roll off, and turned to Karen.

"I'm sorry, Karen," Stick Dog replied. "I don't know what you're referring to."

As he answered, the dad's voice called out, "Thirteen to twelve!"

13-12!

"Jeez, Stick Dog," Karen said. "It is your plan,

you know. You'd think you'd know about it."

"I do have a plan but—" Stick Dog began to say, but he was interrupted. Karen was way too excited to let him finish.

"We know you do, silly!" Karen exclaimed. "That's why I asked if I could ride your horse."

"Umm—"

"Do you know what color it will be?" Karen asked. She had worked herself up into a pretty good frenzy.

"What color what will be?"

"Your horse, silly!" Karen exclaimed. She was hopping up and down now. "I've always wanted to ride a purple horse with pink spots."

"But there's no—"

"Imagine, just imagine. Me on a horse!"
Karen said, and glanced skyward as she
envisioned the prospect. "I can see me now.
There I am up on my purple horse with pink
spots. I'll ride toward a glorious, sinking sun
as it sets in the east! I can't wait!"

"The sun doesn't set in the east," Poo-Poo
corrected.

"It doesn't?"

"No," confirmed Poo-Poo. "It sets in the north."

"That's fine. It doesn't matter," Karen responded. "Nothing matters when I'm galloping away on my horse!"

"Fifteen to thirteen!"

"Almost to twenty-one," Stick Dog whispered to himself. He knew he was running out of time. "Karen, listen. There's no horse in my plan."

"There's not?"

"No."

"But Stripes said there was."

"I, umm, had to change my plan," Stick Dog

attempted to explain. "I couldn't, umm, find a horse anywhere. You know, to, umm, use for my original, horse-centered plan."

"That stinks."

"Yes, I know. I'm disappointed too," Stick Dog said as fast as he could. "But now that I know you've always yearned to ride a horse, I'll, umm, keep that in mind in the future. You know, I'll try to make that happen. I'll look for a horse for you."

"A purple one with pink spots?"

"Yes, a purple one with pink spots."

"Okay, then," Karen said. She still seemed pretty disappointed.

"So, can I tell you my plan?" Stick Dog

asked. "I mean, umm, my new plan. The one that doesn't involve me being a cowboy, lassoing runaway unicorns, and riding a purple horse?"

Mutt, Karen, Stripes, and Poo-Poo all nodded their heads enthusiastically.

Before Stick Dog gave his friends the details of his unicorn-snatching strategy, the dad called out again.

"Sixteen to fifteen!" 16 - 15!

They were running out of time.

CHAPTER 17

THE RISE OF KAREN

Stick Dog spoke quickly.

"I'm going to throw this ball of twine over the branch that the unicorn is tied to," he explained, and pointed. "I'm going to tie the string around Karen's midsection and then pull her up. When she gets high enough, she can bite through the string holding the unicorn and it will fall down."

"I've always wanted to fly!" Karen exclaimed.

Apparently, she already felt better about
not riding a horse today. "Just look at this
streamlined body of mine! I'm a sleek,
torpedo-shaped flying machine! You want
me to fly? Tie me up, Stick Dog! Tie me up!"

Stick Dog gripped that ball of twine in his
mouth again, twisted his head back and to
the left—and then snapped his head forward
and to the right. He released the twine ball
at the greatest point of his forward thrust.

The ball of twine soared
through the air perfectly.
It passed the hanging unicorn—
and reached the apex of its arc above that
thick branch. It then fell down to the ground
among Mutt, Poo-Poo, Karen, and Stripes.

It was a perfect throw.

While the twine ball started and ended its graceful journey through the air, Stick Dog leaped from the top of the picnic table, skipped the bench entirely, and landed on the patio. He hustled toward his friends and got there before the ball of twine even rolled to a stop.

"Sixteen to sixteen!" the dad called.

16 - 16!

Stick Dog heard the score and moved even faster. He knew his very little time was turning quickly into no time at all.

He wrapped the twine around Karen's belly two times as fast as he could.

"Stick Dog?" Poo-Poo asked.

"Yes?" he answered, wrapping the twine a third time.

"How are you going to make sure that Karen doesn't slip out of that string?"

"I'm going to tie a good, strong knot," answered Stick Dog as he began to tie that very knot.

"What kind of knot will you use?"

"Umm, I don't have a name for it," answered Stick Dog honestly. "Just something really secure and safe."

"Hmm," Poo-Poo said with doubt in his voice. "You're not going to use a Rapala Improved-Clinch Non-Slip Loop Knot?"

"Umm. What?"

"You're not using a Rapala Improved-Clinch Non-Slip Loop Knot?"

"Umm, what's that?"

"It's a really, really good knot," Poo-Poo responded authoritatively. "And since, you know, Karen's going to be hanging there and everything, I thought you should tie a really good knot."

This all intrigued Stripes very much. She asked, "How do you know so much about knots, Poo-Poo?"

"I come from a long line of poodle pirates," Poo-Poo said without delay. "And pirates need to use knots all the time. On their boats and whatnot."

"You're kidding?!" Karen said, and took an awkward step closer. Mutt came nearer too.

"Umm, guys? We should really—" Stick Dog tried to say, but he didn't get anywhere. Everyone was way too wrapped up in Poo-Poo's story.

"It's all true," Poo-Poo continued with supreme confidence. "I am descended from a band of powerful poodle pirates. For centuries, my relatives used to rule bodies of water across the globe. Why, you couldn't cast your gaze across an ocean, sea, river,

bay, stream, creek, or puddle without
seeing a poodle pirate marauding about."

From the side yard, the dad called,
"Seventeen to seventeen!"

17-17!

Stick Dog listened as he worked.
He completed the knot, tested its strength,
and hurried back to the picnic table. As

he did, Poo-Poo went on about his pirate ancestors.

"The poodle pirates ruled the waters! Ruled them, let me tell you," he exclaimed. "There was Three-Legged Gus, Two-Legged Jillian, and One-Legged Billy—all famous conquerors and brave beyond brave."

"What did they do?" asked Mutt.

By this time, Stick Dog had retrieved the other end of the twine and wrapped it tightly around his front left paw.

"Oh, you know, the typical pirate-y type things," Poo-Poo answered as Stick Dog kept busy. "Marauding, pillaging, gallivanting—that kind of stuff."

Poo-Poo would have likely continued to talk about his mighty poodle pirate ancestors for some time, but right then something occurred that stole all of their attention.

Karen began to rise up into the air.

CHAPTER 18

THE GREAT WALL OF CHINA

"I'm flying!" Karen exclaimed. She began to flap her short, stubby dachshund legs in the air like wings. "I'm really flying!"

Stick Dog pulled some more on the twine, continuing to wrap it around his front left paw for safety. With each revolution, Karen rose another four or five inches in the air.

In several seconds, she was a few inches above Mutt, Stripes, and Poo-Poo. In fact, her tail brushed across Mutt's forehead as she rose. She was perhaps two and a half feet off the ground now.

"Wow! You guys look so small from up here!" Karen called down, way louder than necessary. "You're like little ants!"

As Stick Dog continued to pull and wrap the twine, he listened to all of Karen's observations—and tried not to laugh.

She was about four feet in the air when

she yelled, "I can't believe this view! It's amazing!"

"What can you see?" asked Poo-Poo.

"Oh, everything!" Karen called back loudly. She was starting to spin a little as she continued her ascent—and this helped her see additional things apparently. "I can see the Eiffel Tower!"

"Where's that?" asked Stripes.

"It's off in the distance! In Mississippi!"

Mutt asked, "What else can you see, Karen?"

She was now about five feet off the ground.

"I can see the Great Wall of China!"

"Where's that?" asked Poo-Poo.

"It's that way," Karen said, and pointed. "In Florida."

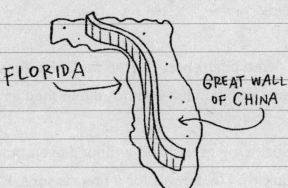

FLORIDA →

GREAT WALL OF CHINA

Stick Dog had to ask, "The Great Wall of China is in Florida?"

"Yes," Karen replied with utter confidence. "For sure."

"I always thought it was, you know, in China," Stick Dog said.

Karen shook her head and replied, "You obviously don't know your geometry as good as me."

"I think you mean geography," said Stick Dog.

"Same difference," Karen said. Her sense of awe and wonder was not diminished at all.

Stick Dog reeled and wrapped even more quickly. He did this for a few reasons. First, he knew they were running out of time. The big male human had just announced the score of their birdie-whacking game again.

It was 19–18. Second, the twine wrapped around his left paw was getting tighter and tighter—and starting to hurt. Karen's safety was his primary concern. He didn't want the twine to cut off his circulation and cause her to fall. And, finally, he still really, really, really wanted to find out if there was something—maybe dessert— inside that unicorn.

In a few more quick wraps, Karen called out again from above.

"Hey, you guys!" she yelled. "Guess what!"

"What?" Mutt called back for all of them.

"You're not going to believe this!"

"What?" Mutt repeated.

"There's a unicorn up here!"

It took a great deal of energy and effort for Stick Dog to resist slapping his forehead when he heard this. He knew if he did, then Karen would fall.

"Karen!" Stick Dog called. "To get the unicorn down all you need to do is bite that twine with your super-sharp teeth!"

The dad yelled, "Nineteen to nineteen!"

19 - 19!

Karen understood Stick Dog's instructions.

She opened her mouth, exposing her canine canines.

She leaned forward.

She was just three inches away from the twine.

Two inches.

One inch.

Until she stopped.

Stick Dog stopped her.

"Karen!" he screamed. "Wait!"

CHAPTER 19

KAREN BITES

Karen closed her mouth.

"What is it, Stick Dog?" she asked. "Why do you want me to stop? Aren't we, you know, in a bit of a rush here?"

"We are!" Stick Dog answered, almost frantically. "But you were about to bite the wrong string!"

"What do you mean?" Karen called down to him from her elevated position. She was about ten feet off the ground now. "The wrong string?"

"You were going to bite the string that's holding you up," Stick Dog explained quickly. "You want to bite the string that's holding the unicorn up!"

"Oops," Karen admitted, and giggled. "I was so enchanted with the spectacular views up here that I guess I wasn't paying attention. How far up am I anyway? Two miles? Three miles?"

"Umm, maybe not quite that much," answered Stick Dog. He cocked his head toward the side yard to listen.

The dad yelled,
"Twenty to nineteen!
Game point!"

20-19!

That was it, Stick Dog
knew. Karen had to
bite that string—the correct string—right
now. He was about to give that instruction,
but Poo-Poo called up to Karen first.

"What can you see now?" Poo-Poo asked.

After squinting her eyes to concentrate all
her visual power and stare out in a southerly
direction, Karen answered, "I can see Santa's
workshop at the North Pole!"

"Karen!" Stick Dog yelped. There was no more time. The humans were playing the possible final point in their birdie-smashing match. "Bite the string! Now!"

Karen bit the string.

And the unicorn started to fall.

CHAPTER 20

HEAD-BASHING

As the unicorn fell, Stick Dog unwrapped the twine from his front left paw as fast as he could. Karen began to make her descent back to the patio.

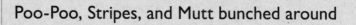

Poo-Poo, Stripes, and Mutt bunched around

the unicorn now that it had smashed down
to the ground beneath the big maple tree.
It settled and leaned at an awkward angle
against the tree trunk. Stripes pawed at
it carefully. Mutt nibbled on the unicorn's
horn. Poo-Poo sniffed at it.

"What's inside?!" Stick Dog asked urgently
as he unreeled the twine even faster. Karen
was almost down to the ground now.

The dad called, "Twenty to twenty!"

20-20!

"What do you mean, Stick Dog?" asked
Stripes.

"Inside the unicorn!" he exclaimed,
unwinding the final loop from around his
paw. He had heard the dad call out the
score. There was only one point to go in
their game. "What's inside the unicorn?!"

"How should I know?" Stripes asked,
dumbfounded. "Do you want me to ask it?
I don't think it will answer, to be honest.
But you never know, I guess."

"It didn't break open?!" Stick Dog asked
incredulously as he leaped toward his
friends. He went
straight toward
Karen. "After that
fall? Seriously?!"

Mutt stopped chewing on the unicorn's horn. He answered, "Nope. Didn't break open, Stick Dog. Doesn't taste too good either."

Stick Dog bit the knot he had secured Karen with and the twine fell off her easily. Then he heard the large male human yell the thing he had been dreading—the thing he really did not want to hear.

"Twenty-one to twenty!"

Stick Dog snapped his head toward the corner of the house. He snapped it back and looked at the fully intact unicorn leaning against the tree. He snapped his head a final time to look at the forest.

He couldn't risk it.

The humans' game was over. They had to leave.

Now.

He would never find out if there was something inside the unicorn or not.

"We have to—" Stick Dog started to say.

But he didn't finish his sentence.

That's because right then the large male human yelled one more thing.

One more miraculous thing.

From the side yard, the dad yelled, "The game's not over yet! The winning team has to win by two points!"

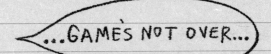

...GAMES NOT OVER...

Stick Dog knew what that meant.

They still had time.

He turned to Poo-Poo.

"Poo-Poo?" he asked.

"Yes, Stick Dog," he answered, lifting his head from the unicorn as he stopped sniffing at it. "Is there something I can help you with?"

Stick Dog asked, "Would you mind bashing

your head into something on purpose?"

"Not at all, Stick Dog," Poo-Poo replied immediately—and proudly. "It is, after all, one of the things I'm best at."

"I know you are."

"What would you like me to bash my head into?"

"The unicorn, if you please."

"Consider it done."

As Poo-Poo backed up to create the proper speed-building distance, the dad called out again.

"Twenty-one to twenty-one!"

Stick Dog, Mutt, Stripes, and Karen backed away from the unicorn.

Poo-Poo lowered his head.

He stiffened his shoulders.

He squinted his eyes.

He stared at his target.

He took off.

He gained speed.

He charged.

He lunged.

He SMASHED into the unicorn.

CHAPTER 21

DESSERT

And the unicorn BURST open.

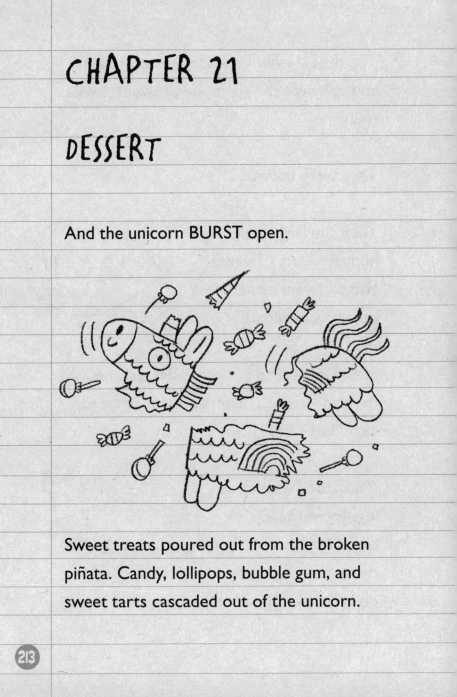

Sweet treats poured out from the broken piñata. Candy, lollipops, bubble gum, and sweet tarts cascaded out of the unicorn.

The dogs—even Stick Dog—stood silent and still over the giant pile of sweet, sweet treasure.

They were in awe.

Then the large male human yelled, "Twenty-two to twenty-one! Next point could win it!"

22-21!

Stick Dog jerked out of his dessert-induced daze and yelped, "Stuff as much as we can into Mutt's fur!"

Mutt stood with his legs spread apart, creating as much candy-carrying space on his body as he could.

Poo-Poo, Stripes, Karen, and Stick Dog pushed, shoved, thrust, and nudged as much of that candy into Mutt's fur as fast as they could.

They had gotten most of it in when the big male human's voice bellowed one last time from around the corner of the house.

"Twenty-three to twenty-one! The kids win!"

THE KIDS WIN!

And Stick Dog yelled one last thing too.

"Go!"

And they went.

They scurried away from the maple tree.

Off the patio.

Across the backyard.

Into the woods.

Through the forest.

And, finally, into Stick Dog's pipe.

When they got there, Mutt gave himself an energetic, vigorous, and massive shake.

And their dessert sprayed everywhere.

The End.

LEARN TO DRAW
STICK DOG & FRIENDS!

DRAWING LESSON #1—STICK DOG

1. Draw a rectangle.

2. Draw a triangle and fill it in.

3. Add another rectangle.

4. Add a smile, a nose, and an eye.

5. Add a tail and legs.

STICK DOG!

DRAWING LESSON #2—POO-POO

1. Draw a rectangle.

2. Draw some squiggles for his ear.

3. Add a rectangle with an opening.

4. Add a nose and an eye.

5. Add a tail and legs and puffballs on the ends.

POO-POO!

DRAWING LESSON #3—STRIPES

1. Draw a rectangle, but
don't connect the
top right corner.

2. Draw a triangle
and fill it in.

3. Add another
rectangle.

4. Add a smile, a nose,
an eye, and lashes.

5. Add a banana for a
tail, legs, and spots.

STRIPES!

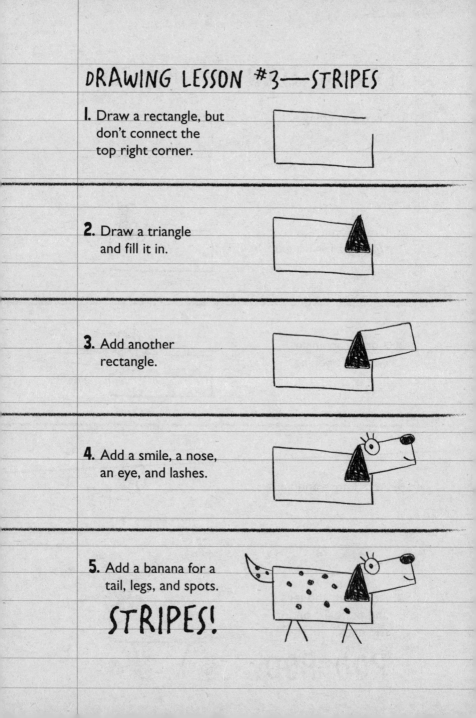

DRAWING LESSON #4—KAREN

I. Draw a long rectangle with an opening on the top right corner.

2. Draw a triangle, but don't fill it in.

3. Add a rectangle with an opening for the mouth.

4. Add a nose, an eye, and eyelashes.

5. Add a tail and legs.

KAREN!

DRAWING LESSON #5—MUTT

1. Draw a rectangle, but don't connect the top right corner.

2. Draw a dinosaur footprint for the ear.

3. You know what's next— a rectangle head with an opening.

4. Add a nose and an eye.

5. Time for a squiggle tail. Add more squiggles to Mutt's body to make him look shaggy.

MUTT!

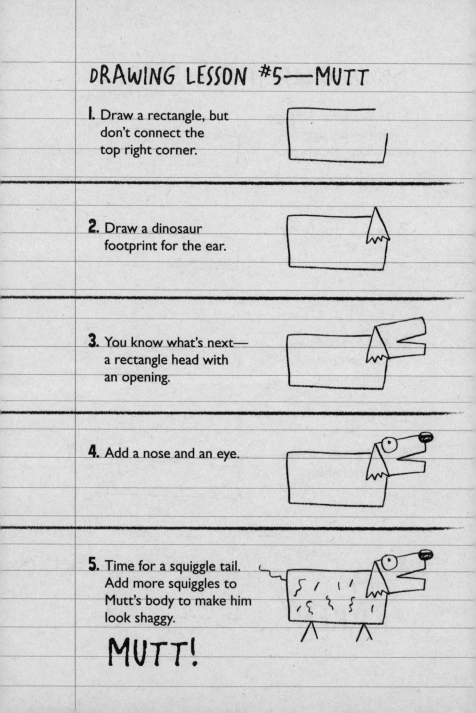

Tom Watson lives in Chicago with his wife, daughter, and son. He also has a dog, as you could probably guess. The dog is a Labrador-Newfoundland mix. Tom says he looks like a Labrador with a bad perm. He wanted to name the dog "Put Your Shirt On" (please don't ask why), but he was outvoted by his family. The dog's name is Shadow. Early in his career Tom worked in politics, including a stint as the chief speechwriter for the governor of Ohio. This experience helped him develop the unique storytelling narrative style of the Stick Dog books. Tom's time in politics also made him realize a very important thing: kids are way smarter than adults. And it's a lot more fun and rewarding to write stories for them than to write speeches for grown-ups.